PASSION REKINDLED

DELANEY DIAMOND

GARDEN AVENUE PRESS

Passion Rekindled by Delaney Diamond

Copyright © 2016, Delaney Diamond

Garden Avenue Press

Atlanta, Georgia

ISBN: 978-1-940636-32-0 (Ebook edition)

ISBN: 978-1-946302-60-1 (Paperback edition)

ISBN: 978-1-946302-22-9 (Audiobook edition)

www.delaneydiamond.com

CHAPTER 1

*S*ylvie Johnson stared at the sketches that one of her in-house designers had brought in. Holding them at arm's length, she examined the drawings of bold oranges and blues planned for next year's spring line. None satisfied her.

"No." She shook her head. "No, no, no." Sighing heavily, she tossed the sketchpads onto the neat desk, a uniquely modern creation she designed herself, made of a slab of glass on top of white concrete legs.

Sylvie glared at Roselle over black designer glasses. "These are horrid. I don't want to see you in my office again until you have something so exquisite I don't regret hiring you." She dismissed the young woman with a tight smile.

"Yes, Miss Johnson."

Roselle grabbed the pads and bowed her head in deference. The act grated on Sylvie's nerves, and she fought the urge to cringe. On more than one occasion she'd told Roselle to stop with the reverential bowing. She wasn't a queen, for heaven's sake, but she also knew that she intimidated the young woman.

Roselle lacked backbone but was sweet. Too sweet. The kind who'd get gobbled up by the vultures of the world if she wasn't careful. She created beautiful designs when pushed, but unfortunately did not dress the part.

Sylvie assessed the young woman with a critical eye. A purple shift dress hung off her bony shoulders, and her narrow face was—with a gray pallor beneath the cinnamon-brown skin—surprisingly gaunt. Roselle looked as if she was not taking care of herself and hadn't eaten in months.

"Roselle," Sylvie called out as the young woman rushed toward the door.

She turned, eyes wide, clutching the sketchpads to her chest.

"Have you eaten today?"

"I...um..."

"I will take that as a no." Sylvie removed her glasses and placed a fist on her hip. "We've talked about this, remember? You must nourish your body or your mind will suffer the consequences. Since I need your mind in tiptop shape—after all, that's what I'm paying for—I need you to take better care of yourself."

"Yes, ma'am," Roselle mumbled.

Sylvie shuffled papers on her desk. "Have Inez order you a meal from the restaurant across the street. Tell her to place it on my bill and order the usual for me, as well."

"Thank you."

In the quiet, Sylvie realized Roselle was still standing in the room. She looked up to find the young woman staring at her with a mixture of adoration and awe.

Sylvie glared at her. "*Go.*"

Roselle darted from the office.

Sylvie shook her head and sank into her soft white chair, the plush fabric molding around her hips and buttocks. She ran three profitable companies from this office, located in Atlanta atop a twenty-story building where she leased fifteen floors and part of the basement.

The entire office contained ultramodern pieces with a feminine twist, stylish but engineered for comfort. The shaggy white chair behind her desk was a very popular item she'd designed, made of ivory sheepskin resting on clear Lucite legs. It went well with the rest of the furnishings, which included white built-in shelves filled with books and awards, and a glass coffee table encircled by a sofa and two armchairs.

Her film development company funded documentaries, a line of office furniture offered high-end pieces made of hearty woods and vibrant fabrics for female executives, and she sold fashion and cosmetics products under the Sylvie brand. She was proud of her accomplishments, but particularly the makeup line, created for women with darker skin tones. Made from natural and organic ingredients, the line had won numerous awards. Reviewers raved that they often forgot they were wearing makeup and swore the products improved their complexions.

She found her notes and scribbled a few items onto her pad, and then went to work drafting a memo on her laptop. Approximately twenty minutes into the task, the intercom beeped.

The voice of her administrative assistant, Inez, came through the speaker. "You have a visitor."

Sylvie lifted a brow at the guarded tone. Her eyes skirted away from the document on the computer to the phone on the corner of her desk. "Who is it?"

"Your ex-husband. Oscar Brooks."

She stiffened.

What was Oscar doing at her office? She couldn't recall the last time he'd been there. Certainly not since they'd divorced and she moved to this new location when her businesses expanded.

With all of their children grown, they had little reason to communicate with each other, and the last time she saw him had been a month ago. They had both attended a function in Miami where their daughter gave a speech. Oscar showed up with one of his young girlfriends, a slight Sylvie made sure he knew she

3

didn't appreciate. They'd had another confrontation when they saw each other at breakfast in the hotel restaurant the next morning, and that had been the last time she'd seen him.

"Miss Johnson, are you there? Should I send him in or...?"

"One moment."

Sylvie went to the gilded oval mirror hanging on the wall and checked her appearance. Perfect. Her raven hair was pulled back from her face, covered in neutral-toned foundation and lipstick to match her dark brown skin.

She straightened the hem of her sleeveless royal blue peplum top and smoothed a hand down the front of the canary trousers before stalking over to the desk. She didn't really care what Oscar thought, but still wanted to look her best. "Send him in."

Sylvie stood behind the desk, posed with a hand on her hip, and took a slow breath, quietly easing air into her lungs as she awaited her ex-husband's entrance.

Oscar entered slowly, dressed in black loafers, jeans, and a dark pullover. His eyes took in the bright room, sun-drenched from the windows covered with sheer drapes at her back, highlighting the white, tan, and splashes of pale rose that filled the expansive room.

The patch of gray hair over his right temple hinted at his age, a man in his fifties. His mother was Brazilian, his father African-American. Some recognized his Latin roots; others mistook the curly hair and swarthy skin for someone of Middle Eastern descent.

He was the kind of person who did his own thing and didn't care what other people thought. One of the many reasons she'd been attracted to him in the first place. He'd been so different from the well-mannered young men she knew that he'd immediately intrigued her.

But right now Sylvie was not intrigued. In fact, she was annoyed because he had disrupted her day.

"You need to shave," she told him, casting a disparaging eye at the shadow of whiskers that covered his chin and jaw. *And a haircut*, she added silently, critically assessing the loose curls on his head. Her eyes avoided the hint of chest hair revealed by the three open buttons on his shirt, and she kept her body still to combat the faint flutter of warmth that seeped into her chest at the untamed virility of his appearance.

Oscar rubbed his palm across the hairs on his jaw, peppered with gray. "I'm my own man. I can do what I want. Have been able to do what I've wanted for fifteen glorious years." He sent a tight smile in her direction.

He crossed his arms over his chest, revealing defined biceps. According to the children, he stayed in shape by regularly going out on his boat. It was obvious he spent a lot of time out there. His face was weathered and sun-kissed from being out in the sun, but he was still very much the young man she had fallen in love with. With a sparkle to his dark brown eyes, and quite handsome.

And she wished she hadn't noticed.

Her nostrils flared. "What do you want?"

"I came to extend an olive branch." He came further into the room, and the skin on Sylvie's neck tightened upon his approach.

"Why?" she asked.

"No need to sound so suspicious. I'm worried about our children, and I want to talk to you about them. Mind if I sit?"

"I'm very busy—"

He dropped into the chair in front of the desk and crossed an ankle over his knee.

"Excuse me, but what are you doing?" Sylvie asked.

"Have a seat, Sylvie, and let's talk."

"Why should I talk to you?"

"Because the only thing you love more than money is our

children. They're the only good thing that came out of our marriage, wouldn't you agree?"

The barb sent a razor-sharp pain through her chest, and Sylvie dropped her gaze to the glass top desk. Regrouping, she compressed her lips and recovered, steeling herself for the conversation with her ex.

She coolly looked at Oscar. "I agree. They're the only good thing."

She sat down across from him.

CHAPTER 2

*O*scar looked thoroughly relaxed in the chair, elbows on the rest, fingers steepled before him. Sylvie, on the other hand, felt tension creep into her muscles, practically invading her bones.

"I'm worried about Ella. I'm sure you know, I came up from Miami for Brett and Natalia's wedding last weekend. I thought I'd see you there," Oscar said.

"I couldn't make it. I sent a gift instead."

She and Oscar could go years without seeing each other, even with four children and mutual acquaintances between them. Brett and Natalia had divorced a few years ago and for some reason reconciled. They were more Oscar's friends than Sylvie's, as she'd steered clear of them ever since she heard rumors that Natalia thought she was a snob. Suspecting Oscar would be in attendance, she'd politely declined the wedding invitation and sent a gift, but only because she liked Brett and found him amusing.

Oscar continued. "I decided to stick around a few extra days and spend time with the girls." "The girls" referred to Ella's daughters, their only grandchildren. "Outwardly Ella seemed fine, but I know my daughter, and I believe it's all a show."

Sylvie had recognized the same and tried to talk to Ella privately, but hadn't gleaned any information of value from her daughter's reticent answers. "Her heart is broken. Her husband left her after their second child was born. Don't worry about Ella. I stay in close contact with her, as well as Simone and the boys."

"Stephan and Reese are not boys," Oscar said.

Sylvie shrugged. "They're my boys, and as far as I'm concerned always will be." Well aware that she treated them differently than Ella and Simone, Sylvie ignored accusations that she coddled her sons and worked too hard on toughening her daughters. The world was a dangerous place for women. Physically as well as emotionally. She refused to allow her daughters to become anyone's prey.

"Since you mentioned Simone, she's my other concern. I ate dinner with her and Cameron, since I didn't get a chance to meet him in Miami." Cameron was their daughter's new boyfriend, and an owner of Club Masquerade, which had the reputation of being the hottest club in Atlanta. "She's upset you won't accept him, and I promised I would talk to you about the situation. He seems like a good man, and I think he'll be good for Simone."

"I'm not convinced. He reminds me too much of someone from my past, who also made bold declarations of love that he didn't mean."

Oscar sat straight in the chair. "If you're talking about me, you and I both know that's BS."

"Really? You left, didn't you?" Their arguments always came back to this. She couldn't help herself.

A muscle in his jaw clenched. "Not even Job could put up with you."

"Until death do us part. Richer or poorer. Better or worse.

Any of that ring a bell, Oscar? Swearing before God and our family and friends." Her blood pressure spiked, heat filling her face and neck.

He leaned forward. "Honor and obey. Any of that ring a bell?" he asked.

Sylvie brushed aside the words with a dismissive sweep of her hand. "Archaic vows that should be stripped from the wedding ceremony."

"And yet you said them, swearing before God and all our family and friends."

Their gazes clashed.

Sylvie stood. "Well, you certainly bounced back, didn't you? With all your little girlfriends."

Oscar stood, too. "We were barely divorced before you took up with that billionaire. The ink was barely dry on our divorce before you flaunted your relationship at the Met Gala, or did you forget?"

"Are you talking about Roger? I did not flaunt anything. He was my escort for the evening." After a very public divorce, she'd needed to save face and her older brother, Cyrus, had suggested the pairing since both she and Roger had received invitations to the exclusive event. "You know, the way you always manage to escort some teenaged trollop to various events."

"They're not trollops, and you know good and well they are not teenagers," Oscar said between his teeth.

"Well, they might as well be, the age difference is so vast." Sylvie held her hands several feet apart to indicate how vast. "And women that young with a man your age. Tsk. Tsk." She sighed, shaking her head. "The game these young women play is so obvious, but men fall for the false interest every time. It would be funny if not so sad."

"What's sad is you sitting in judgment of everyone while you grow old and alone," Oscar spat.

9

The blow of his words reverberated in the room. Sylvie's mouth tightened and her fingers clenched into small fists. "I have plenty of friends and the love of my children. And, as you pointed out, plenty of money to keep me warm. Now, if you'll excuse me, I will show you out. I have several businesses to run, and this impromptu meeting has gone on long enough."

She marched around the desk to escort him from the room, but Oscar grabbed her wrist. Sylvie jerked back from the shocking heat of his touch, but his fingers only tightened. Years had passed since she last experienced his hands on her, their callous texture indicative of the hours he spent on his boat.

His brown eyes flashed. "Is that really all you care about, Sylvie? Money and more of it?"

"I'm just like you. That's all you care about. You married me and made off with a lovely settlement. Twenty-seven million dollars, one and a half million for every year of marriage. You did quite well, wouldn't you say?" Her heart thumped loud and hard against her breastbone.

His jaw went rigid. "I never cared about your money. I cared about you."

"I do *not* believe you, and I will never believe another word that comes out of your mouth. You have no idea what love is. What sacrifice is. You left, after eighteen years. End of story."

"We were fighting night and day—"

"You were fighting with me. I simply wanted—"

"You wanted to tear me down because I wasn't born with a silver spoon in my mouth. When Anthony died—"

"Don't you dare talk about my brother!" This time she managed to yank away her arm. "That coward shot him down like an animal, and when she killed herself, she left my nephew an orphan. She was a selfish, evil cow." More than twenty years later, she still despised the woman who'd stolen her brother so abruptly from her life.

In fact, both of her brothers were dead. Both taken from the earth suddenly and under harsh circumstances. The eldest, Cyrus, died when a drunk driver crashed into his vehicle. Anthony, a gentle musician and her best friend, had been murdered by his wife.

They were both gone. Leaving her alone.

"I can't talk to you about anything, can I?" Oscar fumed. With a disgusted shake of his head, he marched away.

"Yes, go. Leave. You're very good at that."

Back stiffening, he froze halfway to the door. He swung toward her and spoke through thinned, tight lips. "What is the real problem, Sylvie? Is it that I left, or that you couldn't hold on to me?"

Her neck tightened in outrage. "I never wanted to hold on to you."

"No? Every time we talk, you bring up the fact that I left. You throw it in my face. Every. Single. Time. It's been *fifteen* years. When are you going to let go of the anger and accept our marriage is over?"

"I accept it's over, and I paid dearly for the privilege of getting you out of my life."

"Yes, you did, yet you're still not happy." He came slowly toward her, eyes narrowed. "Why is that?"

"What are you suggesting?"

"That maybe all this animosity stems not from anger but from a different place. That maybe you're not as indifferent as you like to pretend."

Sylvie cackled at him, her derisive, high-pitched laughter filling the office. "Oh, Oscar, don't flatter yourself. Run along to one of your little tarts and fill her head with your foolishness. I'm a grown woman and way too intelligent to fall for your silly reverse psychology games."

She turned her back, the movement dismissive. But the next thing she knew, she was being twirled around by Oscar's large hands on her waistline.

Then he kissed her, his mouth landing over hers in a strong kiss.

Shocked, Sylvie stiffened. His hand came up and covered the back of her neck below the thick bun, his clasp warm and firm. The other arm brought her into very close, intimate contact with his hard body, trapping her arms between them.

Shock gave way to pleasure—an overpowering sensation that coursed through her arteries until Sylvie had no choice but to open her mouth beneath Oscar's. His thumb caressed her cheek, as her hand climbed to his face and moved over the surprisingly soft whiskers on his jaw.

His hand swept up and down the sloped curve of her spine, finally easing down to her bottom. Oscar groaned and squeezed, and she felt the hard ridge of his arousal expand against her abdomen.

Sylvie inhaled sharply as heat pooled between her thighs. But she couldn't stop kissing him. Her other hand clutched his collar and she kissed him with urgency, heart tearing through her chest at an alarming rate.

When his tongue sought entrance into her mouth, she allowed it, and the kiss became more demanding. Devouring. Oscar didn't just take command of her mouth. He took command of *all* of her.

Another groan emerged between them, coming from deep in his chest. A masculine rumble of hunger and a demand for more.

As Sylvie eased her fingers up his nape into his hair, her sharp ears picked up the quiet but definite click of the door as it opened.

CHAPTER 3

*S*ylvie pulled back and Oscar immediately released her.

"I'm so sorry, Miss Johnson!" Roselle exclaimed, eyes stretched wide. She held a container of food in her hands.

Sylvie pressed a hand to her chest. "You do not barge into my office! You should always knock."

"I'm sorry. I didn't think. I brought—"

"Get out."

Roselle dashed from the room and the door snicked closed.

Oscar swiped a hand across his mouth. "You didn't have to talk to her like that." His voice sounded hoarse.

"You don't tell me what to do in my office," Sylvie hissed, breathing heavily. Disappointed in her own behavior, she needed to expend her wrath. "And how dare you touch me. You don't—"

"You liked it." He spoke in a matter-of-fact tone.

"I want you out. Now." She moved further away from him and fisted her right hand in helpless frustration.

Oscar's eyes narrowed. "You liked it," he said, his voice a mixture of wonder and shock.

"You took me by surprise."

"I liked it, too," he said in a low voice.

Sylvie stilled. Her body buzzed from his touch. Her nipples tingled, and her inner thighs heated from wanting more of him. "Get. Out."

He didn't move. His eyes ran over her the way they used to. Knowingly. An utterly indecent perusal that signaled exactly what he wanted. What he expected. That type of observation always made her body go up in flames and preceded them making love. Even now, the fiery pulse of blood in her veins made her cheeks flush.

She couldn't move any part of her limbs and barely managed to move her lips to utter the words that would free her from the invisible snare. "Get. Out."

Oscar rubbed a hand over his mouth again and dragged his tongue across his lower lip. He cast one more improper glance in her direction and turned to leave. "I'll be seeing you," he said, as he marched to the door.

The words sounded like a threat when there was no reason for them to see each other again. A threat her body welcomed, blanketing her skin in tingles.

"No, you will not!"

Oscar continued quietly toward the door, his movements slow and precise. At the last moment, he turned, and Sylvie remained in place, holding her breath.

He didn't speak, but kept a narrowed gaze on her for long seconds before he finally exited. When the door closed, the rigidity in her muscles relaxed enough for her to walk stiffly to the desk and collapse into the chair.

With a trembling finger, she pressed a button on the phone and called her assistant. "Inez." She wondered if her assistant could hear the hoarseness in her voice.

"Yes, Miss Johnson."

Sylvie rubbed the back of her neck. Where Oscar had

touched. She still felt his touch. The warmth, the calloused fingers, the firmness of his chest as he crushed her to him.

"Call my masseur. Tell him to drop everything and come right away for an hour-long session."

"Yes, ma'am. Right away. Did you...did you want your lunch?"

"I'll let you know when I'm ready." She couldn't eat a thing now, and more importantly, she didn't want to see or speak to anyone.

Sylvie pressed tentative fingers to her mouth.

How dare he?

She blinked back tears, as a barrage of memories came flooding back. She didn't even know where they came from. The memories simply flooded her, and she snatched two tissues from the box on her desk and dabbed at her eyes.

Memories of amorous kisses. Gentle lovemaking. Years and years of memories that she'd fought and fought and effectively banished from her brain.

How dare he remind her of their past? Of the passion that used to exist between them.

This couldn't be happening. Fifteen years should have been enough. Surely it was sufficient time to forget a man who'd abandoned her. To stop loving him completely.

"Not again," she whispered to the empty room, as wrenching pain twisted through her chest. Sylvie dabbed at her eyes. "Not again. *Please.*" She had to be strong.

She *was* strong.

She'd lost her brother, her best friend and confidant, in a violent murder-suicide. Years later, Oscar left, tearing her world in two. Alive, but unattainable. Unreachable. Untouchable.

Only a couple of years later, her older brother, whom she admired more than anyone else in the world—her encourager, advisor and mentor—was snatched from life by the negligence of a drunk driver. All the men in her life...gone.

Was it any wonder she'd learned to depend on herself?

Sylvie closed her eyes and quietly counted backward. "Ten. Nine. Eight. Seven..."

She continued until she arrived at the number one and then opened her eyes. They were dry, and the tightness in her chest gone.

She straightened her spine and picked up her Mont Blanc pen.

And went back to work.

* * *

AT LEAST SHE didn't slap him.

Oscar's long strides took him across the lobby floor and out into the sunshine. He scanned the busy street filled with cars and people hustling by and decided on a brisk walk to settle his jumpy nerves.

Stuffing his hands into his pockets, he frowned. What had possessed him to kiss Sylvie?

The impulsive move had taken him by surprise as much as it had her, but he'd wanted to kiss her ever since he'd seen her in Miami in her designer dress, breasts sitting high on display and her thick hair piled atop her head, her entire appearance one of majestic refinement.

What surprised him even more than the kiss was the fact that Sylvie didn't push him away. Not at first. She'd kissed him back, and seemed to thoroughly enjoy the mouth-to-mouth contact.

He certainly had.

Oscar smiled to himself. His tongue still hummed with the taste of her, and every inch that he'd touched remained ingrained in his recollection of the charged moment. The soft skin of her neck, the curve of her spine, and the alluring scent of her perfume remained in his nostrils.

His footsteps slowed at an intersection. As he waited for the light to change, his phone rang.

"Hi, Dad." The cheerful voice of his daughter Simone came through the line.

"Hi there, sweetheart, how are you?" Oscar crossed the street with the other pedestrians.

"Fine. Did you get a chance to talk to Mother?"

"I did." Oscar dipped down another busy street toward an Italian restaurant where he could get a bite to eat. Standing with his back to the building, he said, "It didn't go very well."

"Oh." That one little word was filled with disappointment.

"I don't think your mother is going to budge on the situation with Cameron."

Simone sighed heavily. "I want them to get along. I want her to see what a wonderful man he is and how much he makes me happy."

"You can't worry about your mother right now. You need to be concerned about nurturing your relationship with this young man."

"I wish I could do both," Simone murmured.

Oscar watched the people going by on the main street. "Maybe there is something that can be done." With respect to his children, he was just as determined as Sylvie to ensure their happiness. Simone was a grown woman, but he still saw her as his little girl and wanted to fix this problem for her.

"What are you thinking?" Simone asked, sounding hopeful. "Mother can be so difficult."

"Leave your mother to me. You're going to come by later when I join Ella and the girls for dinner?"

Oscar was staying at a hotel while in Atlanta, and Ella had invited him for dinner at her home tonight. His sons were in New York at the moment, but he hoped they'd be back before he returned to Miami.

"I'll be there," Simone said.

"Good. I'll see you later, sweetheart."

Oscar hung up and the phone immediately rang. He cringed when he saw the number and waited a few seconds before reluctantly answering.

"I heard you were in town," she purred.

He pushed down a sigh, running a hand over his head. "Caitlin, listen…"

"I don't want anything. I thought we could meet up for drinks or have dinner and, you know…talk."

"There's nothing to discuss. We had fun, but as I explained to you in Miami, it's over."

"Oscar, are you saying we can't be friends?" she chided.

He rubbed a hand across his jaw.

"Don't tell me friendship is too much to ask," she added.

"No, it's not too much to ask," he said wearily.

"Good! Are you free tonight?"

"Not tonight. How about tomorrow?" he suggested.

She tutted her disappointment. "Fine, but you'll have to make it up to me."

He smiled slightly. "Caitlin…"

"I'm kidding, but it would be nice to get a little gift from you to ease the pain, considering how you dumped me like yesterday's old news."

"That's not what happened. I explained to you why we should end our relationship."

"You explained, but the explanation didn't make sense. We don't need to have everything in common to be compatible. Age is nothing but a number. But anyway, I'm glad you've decided to see me, and I promise to be good. As long as you bring me a little trinket."

He sighed. "All right, Caitlin."

"Thank you! I'll see you tomorrow night."

Oscar hung up and tapped the phone against his palm. This was probably a bad idea, but he needed to make it clear to her that he was no longer interested, and perhaps doing so in person would be the best way to get the point across. Besides, he did feel guilty about the abrupt way he'd ended their relationship after seeing Sylvie in Miami.

He didn't understand how these types of relationships worked, but perhaps a nice parting gift was in order. Thanks to the settlement from Sylvie, he had quite a bit of money at his disposal, but lived well below his means and hardly spent any of it.

His thoughts turned once again to Sylvie, recalling the day she agreed to marry him—the elation he felt that this magnificent creature, a woman so lovely and from a family whose legacy could be traced to the slave ships that carried her ancestors to the shores of the Caribbean, had agreed to become his wife. He'd been so overwhelmed, like a man who'd won the jackpot.

Walking to the restaurant, Oscar pinpointed two goals he must achieve before he left Atlanta.

The first was to get Sylvie's blessing for Simone and Cameron.

The second was to determine if Sylvie really hated him or not.

CHAPTER 4

This was Oscar's first visit to Sylvie's penthouse. During their marriage, they'd lived in a mansion north of the city. With all of their children grown and in their own homes, it made sense Sylvie had downsized to a more manageable property closer to her office.

His daughter had spoken to Sylvie's housekeeper, who in turn spoke to security at the front desk, which allowed him to charm his way past the lobby to the top-level condominium. When Oscar exited the elevator into the vestibule of Sylvie's penthouse, her housekeeper, Trevor, appeared in his uniform, a gray top and gray pants to match the gray hair on his head.

A smile expanded across his leather-colored face. Only a very special kind of person could put up with Sylvie's exacting nature, and Trevor was one of the best. In truth, he managed Sylvie, though she'd never admit it.

"Mr. Brooks, it's good to see you," he said, clasping both of Oscar's hands in his.

"Likewise." Oscar gave the other man's hands a solid shake. "It's been a long time."

Trevor nodded. "Too long. I believe the last time was at Ella's wedding."

"It was."

"Would you like me to announce you now?" Trevor asked.

"I would. She doesn't know I'm here?"

"Not yet, sir."

"This should be interesting."

Another smile crossed Trevor's lips, but he was too polite to laugh outright. "I'll take you into the sitting room."

Trevor escorted Oscar across the sparkling mahogany floors to a room filled with white carpet, so thick he felt the softness under his feet, even through his shoes. The room was decorated in a neutral palate of alabaster and dove gray, with two loveseats and a chaise lounge in front of a fireplace. With Sylvie's great eye for design, the room appeared comfortable but chic.

A decades-old photo of her and her brothers sat in a silver frame on a side table. She stood between the two of them, all three dressed in formal evening attire. Cyrus, her austere older brother, smiled into the camera—one of the few times Oscar actually recalled seeing such outright amusement on his face. He'd always been very protective of his sister and the family name. Sylvie held on to his arm, her face cloaked with joy as she rested her head against the arm of her younger sibling, her brother Anthony. Anthony, the violinist, whose kind eyes crinkled at the corners as he laughed. The untimely, violent death of he and his wife had decimated the Johnson family.

Photographs of Oscar's two granddaughters sat in silver frames on another table, but his eyes shifted and settled on the family portrait on one wall. Sylvie, Stephan and Reese, Simone and Ella, and Ella's daughters graced the professional photo, all of them dressed in white. It appeared to be a complete family. Without him.

Pain screwed into Oscar's chest, right at the spot where his heart beat under his ribs.

"What are you doing here?"

Sylvie's imperial-toned question jolted him from his personal funk, and Oscar turned to see her looking very relaxed in a black long-sleeved tunic and ivory slacks.

"Hello, Sylvie."

Her mouth tightened and her very expressive eyes flashed at him. They were an unusually light shade of brown and a hue she shared with her two brothers, a notable contrast against the dark walnut color of her skin.

"How did you get up here? I need to speak to security about allowing people up without my permission."

"Trevor arranged for me to come up."

"Then I need to speak to Trevor. He should know better." She straightened her shoulders. "You didn't answer my question. What are you doing here? You're not going to kiss me again, are you?"

Oscar didn't answer right away, noting the tension in her body. As usual, she was immediately confrontational, but he'd promised himself he would not get drawn into another battle with her. That was exactly what she wanted. Purposely combative, she constantly picked fights with him. He would remain calm—even if he developed an ulcer doing so.

He walked toward her and her body stiffened even more, guarded eyes watching him closely. "I'm not going to kiss you again. Unless you want me to?"

Her face cemented into a stony mask, but her pupils dilated at the softly asked question.

"I. Do. Not."

Oscar's eyes dropped to the pulse in her throat, which beat at a surprisingly fast rate. "Then we can talk without interruption, specifically about Simone. We never finished that conversation."

"Because you kissed me. You had no right to do that."

He remained calm but observant. She appeared agitated, at a

loss to know what to do with her hands. She clasped and unclasped them, and then clasped them again. If he didn't know better, he'd say Sylvie was nervous.

"You're correct. I didn't."

She compressed her lips as she regarded Oscar. "What are you up to?"

"I need a little bit of your time. To talk about Simone and Cameron. That's not too much to ask, is it?" He smiled in a disarming way. If he simply played nice, he'd wear her down. He hoped.

"No, I suppose not," she said slowly, eyes narrowing. "What exactly did you want to discuss about them?"

Oscar sat in one of the chairs. "Have a seat. We're not adversaries. At least, we don't have to be."

"We have been for the past fifteen years."

"Maybe we should end that, don't you think?"

In lieu of answering, she sat in the other chair, catty-corner to the one he chose. She eyed him warily. "What brought about this change?"

"I've never thought of you as an adversary," Oscar admitted.

"Not even during the divorce?"

"Well, maybe a little bit back then, but like I said, it's been a long time. Fifteen years."

She swallowed. "Are you suggesting we become friends?"

"I don't know that we could ever become friends, but we can at least be civilized."

"For the sake of the children?"

He paused. Their offspring didn't seem like a good enough reason. For years he'd thought he didn't care anything about Sylvie. His ego had been bruised when she took up with that billionaire so soon after their divorce. It was as if she'd said good riddance. Look at me, I can do so much better than you. He'd nursed a broken heart, while she'd moved on to someone better suited to her lifestyle and socioeconomic level.

"For the sake of our children and our grandchildren," Oscar said.

She brushed imaginary lint from her pants leg but didn't respond, and as he considered her, he thought back to the early days of their marriage. For the past fifteen years, he hadn't met anyone like Sylvie Johnson.

"Why don't we try being civilized and see what happens?" he suggested. "I'll go first. I saw the documentary you funded on child brides. Very informative and opened my eyes about the practice."

Sylvie licked her lips, moistening her full mouth and reminding him of how much he'd enjoyed kissing her the other day. He shifted to alleviate the tightness in his groin.

"It's a very important topic. The fundraiser was a smashing success. The money we raised will help build awareness about the practice and fund economic and education initiatives for the girls who participated in the documentary, and many others."

"That's great."

"You can't imagine the stories I heard from the producers. What we shared was only a small fraction of what happens to those young girls."

Before long, she was explaining in detail exactly which programs the money would be donated to and how it would help the girls and their communities. Oscar listened with rapt attention, nodding occasionally and at other times asking pointed questions. Sylvie visibly relaxed, to the point where she forgot to be on guard.

He became riveted as she spoke with such passion about the subject. But that was typical of his ex-wife. A passionate person by nature, she tackled every task with single-minded fervor. She loved hard, in a no-holds-barred fashion. If Sylvie Johnson loved you, she would move heaven, Earth, and the entire universe to not only give you whatever you needed, but protect you to the best of her ability. You became her focus, and no one dared hurt or damage someone she loved.

He'd been someone she loved once, and the loss burned to the depths of his soul.

The room was filled with pictures of the people she passionately loved, protected, and cared for. Her brothers. Their children and grandchildren.

Oscar stood abruptly, forcing Sylvie to break off in the middle of a sentence. He stalked to the fireplace. "So, about Cameron," he said in a brusque tone.

Sylvie blinked. "What would you like to discuss about Cameron?" she asked.

"I promised Simone I would talk to you about giving him a chance. She told me what you did."

She'd gone to visit Cameron at his home, making sure he understood that she thought he was not only wrong for her daughter, but he was doing himself a disservice by getting involved with someone so wealthy.

For a split second, Sylvie dropped her eyes to her lap. "Simone made it very clear she wasn't happy with me for what I did. I apologized to her."

"What about apologizing to Cameron?" Oscar asked.

"I—"

"Do you understand what you did was wrong?"

Sylvie frowned at him. "Why are you talking to me in that tone of voice?" She rose to her feet. "I will always do whatever I need to do to protect my children."

"You weren't protecting her. You meddled in her personal relationship and almost destroyed it before it even got started."

"I don't need you to chastise me," she said.

"Somebody needs to," Oscar said.

"Who do you think you are? You showed up at my house uninvited, and now you want to tell me what to do?"

"Yes. I do. Because I don't think you realized how much pain your words could cause. You go around making accusations and snide comments and then climb into your ivory tower at the top of the building without a care in the world. Meanwhile, you've decimated the person you attacked."

"I think decimate is a bit harsh. I—"

"I asked you a question. Do you even know what you did wrong? Can you admit that you did something wrong?"

"I told you that I apologized to Simone," she said flippantly.

"And what about Cameron? Did you apologize to him?" Her cavalier attitude infuriated Oscar more than it should, but he didn't even know why. "That young man should not have been treated that way. He deserves an apology. You *owe* him an apology."

Her brows snapped together. "Why are you so worked up about Simone's boyfriend?"

"Because…" Yes, why? Why so heated? And then Oscar understood the deeper reason why he was working so hard to fix this mess. Because he hadn't been able to fix his own marriage. Because he'd felt he deserved an apology and never received one. "He's a human being, Sylvie. Just because he's not someone who you love doesn't mean he should be treated with less respect. You had no business interfering in their lives."

"For someone who's insistent I had no business interfering, you certainly have no problem doing so yourself."

"Because that young man deserves respect."

"I did not disrespect him."

"Yes, you did. I can only imagine the way you spoke to him, with your nose in the air and condescension in your voice. You're very good at it. I know you didn't give him any respect, because I've been there. I'd bet a million dollars you treated him with the same lack of respect you treated me."

Instead of arguing or denying, Sylvie stared at Oscar, well-formed brows low over her eyes. That was when he realized he'd yelled the last few sentences.

Trevor appeared in the doorway. "Is everything all right in here, Miss Johnson?" he asked.

"Yes, Trevor, I'm fine." Sylvie dismissed her employee with a soft smile, and the housekeeper stared across the room at Oscar, clearly regretting his decision to allow him into the house.

Oscar couldn't blame him. He greatly regretted his decision to come.

CHAPTER 5

*W*hen they were alone again, Sylvie cleared her throat. "You thought I didn't respect you?"

"You didn't." The words came out clipped and bitter. "You changed after your brother was murdered. You don't like to talk about it, but that's exactly what happened. The change was gradual. At first I thought you were just grieving, but you became someone else. Angrier. Bitter. Eventually, you made it very clear that the house *we* lived in was *your* house, and the money you'd inherited and earned allowed us to live a very specific lifestyle that *I* could never afford." His face twisted into a snarl of anger, and he turned away from her.

Shamed into silence, Sylvie watched her ex-husband's stiff body and the way he dragged a hand down his face. Moving on quiet feet, she walked over and placed a hand on his shoulder blade. Oscar twisted around swiftly, his eyes wide and startled, as if he couldn't believe she'd reached out to him.

She dropped her hand and let the fingers curl at her side. "I'm sorry I gave you the impression that I didn't respect you. I respected you, Oscar. You're an excellent father. You were a good husband, until I ruined our marriage—"

"Sylvie…"

She stepped back and held up her hands. "No. Let me finish." She searched the room and pulled strength from the photos of her brothers and children. When her eyes rested on Oscar again, she sensed he wanted to speak, but at the same time, he wanted to hear the words she had to say. Taking a deep breath, Sylvie forged on, facing her actions for the first time in a very long time. "You think our marriage started falling apart after my brother died, but that's not exactly what happened. Anthony's death destroyed me. I can't deny that." She rubbed her hands together, a ghost of pain brushing over her chest. "I was very close to him. To both of my brothers, but in different ways. We were unique in the world, and it made us closer, because it was rare to see black faces with our level our wealth.

"Cyrus was the strong one, the smart one, the leader, the crown prince of the family empire. I learned so much from him. While Father often made remarks about me getting married and having babies, Cyrus insisted that if I wanted to work, I should be able to. 'Options,' he used to say. 'Give yourself options, Sylvie.'"

Oscar smiled when she lowered her voice in an effort to imitate her brother.

"His advice and encouragement enabled me to become the businessperson I am today. Anthony, however, was different— as you well know. He didn't care much for business." Sylvie walked over to the photo of the three of them in evening attire, laughing and smiling. Emotion tightened her throat, but after a few moments, she spoke again. "He was so gentle and kind, but fiercely protective of me, even though he was a year younger. He played several instruments, but you know how much he adored that violin." She shook her head, passing a finger over her brother's smiling face. "He was my best friend, and…when he died, it was just so unfair."

"Sylvie, don't upset yourself."

She waved away Oscar's concern, faced him, and took a strengthening breath. "My poor nephew, Trenton, was left all alone without a mother or a father. And do you know his mother's people, those horrible people, cared nothing about that boy? Nothing at all! They claimed to want him, but all they wanted was his trust fund."

"You don't know that. You—"

"I am not mistaken. I *know*." She hesitated at the brink of sharing a private matter she'd kept to herself for decades. Quietly, she said, "As you know, Cyrus and his wife took Trenton in. But what you don't know is that his uncle—his mother's brother—and his wife tried to get custody of him. Cyrus doubted their sincerity but didn't want a court battle playing out in the press. My nephew had been through enough, and he needed therapy after seeing such violence. He needed to be a child and have fun. We could not risk him going to those people. They knew our family would provide for him and whoever was his guardian. He was, after all, our brother's son. So Cyrus offered them money, to stay out of the boy's life. One would think that they would curse at Cyrus because such an offer would be offensive. Perhaps they would tell my brother where he could stick his millions. Or even hesitate and need time to think, because while they wanted the child, millions of dollars is a moral temptation that any reasonable person would find difficult to resist. But do you know the first thing they did?"

Slowly, Oscar shook his head.

Sylvie enunciated every word, so there was no misunderstanding. "Those people *demanded* a higher sum. As if...as if my nephew were chattel."

Oscar flinched. "Sylvie, I'm sorry. I had no idea."

"Cyrus, his wife, and I were the only family members who knew the truth." She inhaled deeply. "Cyrus gave them what they asked for. He didn't care. He would have given them more if they'd asked. Cyrus and Constance took Trenton in, treating him like he was their son, exactly the same as their other children. He is their son. Bought and paid for," she said bitterly.

"Don't say that."

"Why not? It's true. That's when it started, Oscar. My eyes opened to the ugliness of the world. First Anthony was taken from us, and then the way those people handed over Trenton without a fight, for money. I would give up everything for my children. Everything." She smoothed a hand over her hip. "That incident made me fully understand I could buy anything I wanted. Smiles, friendships, acceptance."

Oscar studied her. "And you started to wonder if you'd bought yourself a husband."

Pain twisted inside her chest as the accusation hit home. "I..." Words failed her, because his assessment was true.

He came closer. "You became disappointed. Anthony was no longer here to comfort and encourage you, to allay your fears. To neutralize the cynicism with a positive spin. You assumed I was like everyone else, and my true colors would eventually show."

"You were in sales, which meant you know the right things to say, in my opinion. I couldn't be sure anymore." Back then he worked for a boat dealer selling new and used vessels. He concentrated on luxury brands, which was how they'd met. Sylvie had accompanied a friend when Oscar had taken them out to test a boat. That day, her friend bought a boat, and Oscar got her phone number.

"You felt I had sold you a fairytale, and I would eventually leave. So instead of sticking around until that happened, you pushed me away."

"It wasn't a conscious decision," Sylvie said. She took out her pain, disappointment, and anguish on him.

"Pushing me away didn't work, though, did it?" After all

31

she'd put him through, how could his eyes be so kind when he looked at her? "The hurt is still there. The fear of abandonment."

"I am fearless," she said quietly.

"Yes, you are. Strong, fearless, intelligent. All traits I admired in you. Still do." He swallowed. "We were good together once, you and I. For a little while, we had a good life. Do you ever think about that? About us?"

Sylvie emphatically shook her head. "I don't want to remember," she said with a quiver to her voice. "Stop."

"Why?"

"Because you left!" she reminded him.

"You asked for a divorce, and I was tired," he said, his voice also raised.

"So then why are you here now?" she demanded. "We can discuss Simone over the phone. What do you want, Oscar, because I know you want something."

He didn't respond right away. His gaze flicked around the room, jaw hardening as if he fought back an abundance of emotion. Finally, he crossed the plush carpet and took her hand.

"I've tried, but..." He heaved a deep sigh and pressed his mouth to her wrist in a gentle, careful caress. The pulse beneath her skin jumped to life. "I can't stop thinking about you," he whispered, voice raw. Sylvie remained frozen as he came even closer and placed the same gentle caress to her forehead. "I remember all the good times."

Her heart ached as the memories she'd expunged from her mind came flooding back. Their first date, and how nervous Oscar had been when he met her parents and brothers. The tears of joy they cried together at the birth of every single one of their children. The anniversary they spent at the lake house all alone, cut off from family and friends—just the two of them. Family vacations around the world, and so many other memories they could fill a thousand photo albums.

"I remember all the good times, too," she admitted.

"Oh, Sylvie." A smile softened his face, and he cradled her cheek in his hand. She leaned into the rough texture of his palm. His head bent, hesitantly at first, and when she didn't withdraw, he kissed her, plucking her lower lip between his teeth. The gentle abrasion sent an erotic thrill through her body.

"You said you weren't going to kiss me again," she whispered.

"Unless you want me to," he reminded her.

He kissed the corner of her mouth, and the tip of her tongue flicked out to taste him.

"I never said I want you to," she said.

"It's obvious you do."

They shared a proper kiss. No teasing, but mouths meeting in a hungry, moist pull and tug. Her arms slipped around his neck, and her breasts pressed flat against the hard plane of his chest. Her body came alive again, just as it had in her office—in a way she hadn't experienced in years.

A delicate moan escaped as they devoured each other, their bodies flattened as they sought closer contact.

"Oh god, Sylvie, I want you so much. Let me…" Oscar's lips against her neck coaxed a helpless moan from her lips, but Sylvie pressed a restraining hand against his chest.

Dropping her gaze, she said, "It's been a long time, Oscar."

"How long?"

Her eyes met his. "Two years, almost," she said softly.

He traced her cheek with a forefinger. "I'm not that far behind. Over a year for me."

Sylvie gasped. "What about the girl at the event in Miami?" she asked.

Oscar shook his head. "I booked her a room for the night and bought her a ticket home to Atlanta for the next day. I took a separate room at the hotel, and the next morning sat at breakfast hoping for a glimpse of you."

"Goodness." Sylvie covered her mouth with a hand, and then

moved it to touch his cheek. "Then I came down, and the minute you approached, I attacked."

"You attacked."

"Oh, Oscar..."

"Shh. Enough regret. Enough about mistakes." Dark brown eyes scoured her face. "I don't want to think about that anymore. We still have chemistry, and we're both here. So what do you think?" His thumb stroked her jaw line. "Can I spend the night?"

The room whirled in a dizzying tilt as Sylvie considered the question. Finally, she nodded. "Yes, Oscar. I would very much like you to stay the night."

CHAPTER 6

Decorated in her favorite color, white, Sylvie's bedroom was as neat and opulent as the rest of the condo. A grand king bed, covered in white linens and with a tufted dove gray headboard, hugged the middle of the room.

Oscar stood beside the cushioned bench at the foot of the bed and removed pins from Sylvie's hair. She fidgeted in front of him. He was nervous, too, after so long apart.

"Why do you always wear your hair up?" When they were married, she used to wear it down most of the time. Not long after the divorce, he noticed she wore her hair up more often than not.

"It's so thick and unruly and just easier this way." Breathy nervousness filled her voice.

"I used to brush it for you." He lifted out another pin.

One by one, Oscar removed the clips and pins, and set them on the bench at the foot of the bed. He combed his fingers through her thick hair until it spread out around her shoulders like spun black silk.

"Where's your brush?"

"In there." She pointed at the half-open door, which led the way into her dressing room. He retrieved the brush and came back, and Sylvie sat on the bench. He brushed her hair, smoothing each strand from her face with gentle strokes all the way down to the middle of her back.

She kept her eyes downcast, fingers curled in her lap.

"Do you want me to stop?" Oscar asked.

"No, please don't," she said softly.

He continued his ministrations until the tension eased from her body. By then, he burned with anticipation.

He swept the mass of hair over one shoulder and brushed the back of her neck with his lips, sucking until a whimper escaped her throat and she angled her neck, yielding greater access. One hand slid beneath the tunic and cupped her breast-filled satin bra. She let out another strangled whimper, and the sound of her pleasure prompted him to flick his thumb back and forth across the taut nipple.

They stood at the same time, and he led her to the bed. They lay down, facing each other for a while.

"Are you sure?" Oscar asked.

"Yes. I'm sure. I've missed you." She bit her bottom lip, as if she immediately regretted the admission, but he didn't let her take it back. Moving slowly, Oscar covered her body with his.

"I've missed you, too, my love."

Her eyes fluttered closed as he whispered the old endearment, and he took that moment to give her another kiss, foregoing the easy coaxing from before and swooping his tongue into the sweet depths of her mouth. He could never get enough of her taste or the alluring scent of her skin.

They quickly undressed, and with each article of clothing Oscar removed, he became more anxious. Sylvie had changed and matured, but she was still a beautiful woman, with deep walnut skin and full breasts capped by mahogany nipples. Heat flared in his loins when she looped her arms around his neck. He trailed gentle kisses down her jaw to the sensitive line of her throat. Fiery hunger came alive in him—hunger that urged him to claim and possess all that he'd lost.

"Oscar," Sylvie whispered.

The press of him between her legs was a welcome weight. She arched her back and ran a foot up and down Oscar's hair-roughened leg. Sweeping a hand down his chest, she traveled over old, familiar territory. Hair covered his torso down to his pelvis. He was so masculine—not overtly muscular, but with a firm body and tight arms.

Oscar reacquainted himself with her, too, in a much more thorough fashion. He used his preferred method—moving his mouth down her body, dragging his tongue across her stomach and hips, and lodging a gentle nip between her legs. The intimate kiss inflicted a surge of heat at her groin and she squirmed, an involuntary gasp escaping her lips.

He went lower, incorporating his teeth. Against her calves, using delicate little nibbles. Against her ankles, sucking with intensity. The loving attack inflamed her skin wherever he touched.

When he came back up, Sylvie trailed her fingers over the silken length between his legs, tracing the throbbing flesh with exploratory fingers until he inhaled a sharp breath and muttered a guttural curse, thrusting against her hand.

"Sylvie," he groaned. His dark eyes flashed with incendiary passion.

Cupping her breasts, he tongued one engorged nipple. He moved with impatience, worrying the breast and its tip and pressing his tongue against the taut flesh before transferring his attention to the other. She made a soft noise and wiggled beneath him, threading her fingers into his curly mane and arching into the moist sucking of his mouth. Her stomach tightened as she lifted her hips to his and rubbed her aching body against the hardness that prodded between her thighs.

Oscar slid a hand up the inside of her leg and fondled the

center of her. Stroking the sensitive knot of nerves until she begged, pleaded for relief from the painful ache of arousal.

"Are you ready for me, my love?" he whispered into her neck, pushing her knees apart.

"Yes." She barely got the word out. Her voice shook as it left her lips.

He lifted his head to look down at her, and with a simple forward motion, notched his body into hers. Sylvie's mouth fell open. The sensation was indescribably good. She felt so full. She forgot to breathe. Forgot to think. Torso to torso, the hairs on his chest tickled the tips of her breasts.

Then his hips started thrusting slowly. He kept one hand between them and stroked her clit as he moved in and out. Pleasure mounted in her loins and Sylvie sank her nails into his flexing ass. She never wanted him to stop. Never ever wanted to lose this feeling.

She ran her hands up his back, smoothing her palms over warm skin. He lowered his head and kissed her again, tongues tangling, their rapid, shallow breaths mingling.

Oscar moved with greater speed. Each time she lifted up, he pressed down. He moaned her name, gripping her ass and lifting her from the bed to plunge deeper—all the way to the hilt. Broken breaths beat the side of her neck, and Sylvie held on tight, determined to keep up as he increased his speed.

With a harsh growl, Oscar gripped a handful of her hair and pounded faster. Each thrust sliced through her body, hard silk withdrawing and then gliding back in.

The orgasm hit like an atomic explosion and her eyes clamped shut. Buffeted by a storm of sensation, Sylvie cried out, clawing at his back. She rode the waves of a consuming climax that surged and ebbed throughout her body.

Thrusting several more times, Oscar exploded. His entire body tensed, his fingers tightening in her hair right as he let out a deep groan, and then collapsed.

With a heavy sigh, he rolled with her in his arms, kissing her face and smoothing her hair with gentler fingers. He moved to ease away, but Sylvie kept her arms around his neck and legs around his waist. She refused to let him pull out.

Oscar understood what she couldn't say. She needed a little more time—wanted to stay this close a little bit longer.

He kept his arms around her and drizzled kisses on her brow and nose. And for a long time they stayed that way, wrapped in each other's arms. Even after their breathing returned to normal.

CHAPTER 7

*R*unning a few minutes late, Sylvie exited the elevator onto the floor where her office was located. The pristine waiting area contained some of her luxurious designs mixed with the contemporary line of a manufacturer whose pieces she admired.

"Good morning," she said to Inez.

"Good morning, Miss—" Inez looked up from the computer, and her mouth fell open.

Sylvie stopped beside her assistant's desk. "Is something the matter?" she asked.

Inez blinked, as if to clear her vision. "I—Your hair is different."

"I thought I'd try something new." Sylvie trailed her fingers through the strands, which hung in soft waves onto her shoulders and back. "What do you think?" A tiny knot appeared in her stomach.

She was running behind because she'd called her stylist and instructed him to give her a different look with her hair down. He'd parted it in the middle, flat-ironed it straight, and then added texture with a large-barrel curling iron.

Inez examined her. "I like it. A lot, actually. You look different. If I may say…softer."

"Softer?"

"Yes, ma'am." Inez's teeth sank into her red lips, her blue eyes containing hesitation, as if worried she'd said too much.

"Younger?" Sylvie suggested, with a raised brow.

Inez, close in age to Sylvie, smiled and nodded. She wore her own hair medium length and streaked with gray. "That, too."

"Hm. Thank you."

Sylvie marched into her office, but allowed herself a private, self-satisfied grin. Practically, she couldn't imagine wearing her hair like this every day, but the style was a nice change.

She stood in front of the mirror on her wall, examining her face for a few seconds. As Inez pointed out, there was a softening of her features, but she couldn't attribute the difference solely to a new hairstyle. In fact, if she had to assign credit, the change her assistant saw assuredly came from within and manifested on the outside.

Oscar had not only spent Wednesday night at the penthouse, he'd spent Thursday night there, too. This morning he'd left early so he could get back to his hotel room and get ready for a meeting with a potential boat buyer. He didn't have to work, but with his vast knowledge, he occasionally brokered deals between wealthy clients.

They spoke while she rode to work, and from their conversation, she had the distinct impression that Oscar intended to see more of her. A lot more. Frankly, she wanted to spend more time with him, too.

With a busy morning planned, Sylvie finally sat down and went to work. She participated in a conference call about a new film project, agreed to an interview with an entertainment magazine to discuss the advantages of shooting movies in Georgia, and then settled into sketching furniture ideas.

Midmorning, Roselle came in with a fresh take on the spring clothing designs, which Sylvie loved.

"This is more like it," she said.

Roselle beamed. "I'm so happy you're pleased, Miss Johnson."

Sylvie dropped the pad on the desk. "You do good work, but I need to you to care as much about your own appearance as you do these designs."

Roselle's face fell, and so did her gaze. "Yes, ma'am," she mumbled.

"Roselle." The young woman's eyes flicked up. "You must learn to take criticism. If you can't take criticism, you can't grow."

"Yes, ma'am."

Sylvie placed a fist on her hip. "First of all, you need a makeover. I don't have to tell you that. I'm sure you know. The sooner the better, because I can't have you accompanying me to events looking like this." Today's outfit was a shapeless skirt and large blouse that looked like a fashion travesty from 1980.

Roselle's eyes widened. "You want me to—to attend industry events with you?"

"Well, yes. Unless you think I should take someone who's less qualified."

"No, please...I..." She stopped in an effort to control the flow of words. "I would be honored," she managed in a whisper, one hand pressed to her chest.

"Well then, we must do something about your appearance. You've been eating, I assume?" Sylvie asked, as she hit the intercom on the phone.

"Yes, I have," Roselle assured her.

"Inez, I need you to set a few appointments with our contacts at several boutiques. Roselle is going shopping."

"High end or mid-range?"

Sylvie pursed her lips. "High end. Please make sure Neville understands he cannot hand over Roselle to just anyone, the way he did June two months ago. That young woman did not know how to dress for June's size and shape, and I don't want the same for Roselle. If we have another fiasco like that, I will take my business elsewhere."

"Yes, Miss Johnson."

"Also, call Regina at the salon and tell her I need a cut, style, color, and makeup tutorial for Roselle early next week." She hung up.

Roselle clasped her hands. "Thank you, Miss Johnson. I don't know what to say."

"Thank you is enough, but I'm not giving you anything. I'm merely subsidizing your wardrobe. You will pay me back twenty-five percent of the final bill. You must be willing to invest in yourself. I'm giving you a hand up, not a handout."

"Yes, ma'am."

Sylvie put on her glasses and tapped her computer awake. From the corner of her eye, she saw Roselle still standing in the room. "Was there something else?" she asked.

"Why are you doing this for me?" Roselle asked quietly.

Sylvie thought for a moment. It was not uncommon for her to reward deserving employees. She looked for ones who had potential. "I'm investing in you. I believe in you. Do you believe in yourself?"

Roselle grimaced and made an unintelligible sound.

"That's a problem," Sylvie said. "You're a hard worker and very talented. The only thing separating you and anyone else from success is confidence. You lack confidence, and I'm going to help you get it. Society would like us to believe our outward appearance doesn't matter, but that's poppycock. The right clothes, hair, and makeup can do wonders for your confidence and the way people treat you. It shouldn't matter, but it does. *C'est la vie*. So, from now on, you are going to dress the part of a confident fashion designer. Head up, back straight, shoulders back."

Before her eyes, Roselle straightened and lifted her head. Even in the unattractive clothes, the change in posture made a difference in her appearance.

"Thank you, ma'am." Roselle walked toward the door.

"Roselle." The young woman paused, and Sylvie watched her over her glasses. "You can't control what people say, but you can control how you react to their words. Don't ever let anyone make you feel bad about yourself. Not even me. Do you understand?"

Roselle nodded. "Yes, ma'am." With a grateful smile, she quietly left.

Sylvie went back to work. At a knock on the door, she looked up from the desk to see Oscar enter. The sight of him in a pair of dark denims with his face shaved and curls tamed by gel sent shivers shimmying up her inner thighs, forcing her to squeeze her legs together to squelch the sensation.

"Has everyone in my employ fallen under your spell? How in the world did you get in here?"

"Don't blame Inez. I charmed my way in," Oscar said, striding across the floor.

"What are you doing here?" She watched as he walked around the desk.

"I came to take you to lunch." He dropped a kiss to her lips.

Sylvie blinked, taken aback.

Oscar had always been openly affectionate—with the children, with her. He gave the best hugs. He didn't pull you into an embrace. He *enveloped* you, and rubbed your back. His hugs were an experience, like an all-over body massage.

She'd had to get used to such displays when they first started seeing each other, having grown up in a household where her parents seldom exhibited outward displays of affection. While she didn't doubt their love, she'd never experienced kisses and hugs and frequent words of love from them. They'd been too busy teaching the proper way to sit or stand and building up her confidence by reminding her that as a black child, she was just as intelligent and valuable as anyone else—male or female.

She'd learned to appreciate Oscar, who touched and kissed her constantly, not only in a sexual way, but to express tenderness. Until that very moment, Sylvie had forgotten how much she'd missed those gestures, and by virtue of that thought alone, she looked forward to lunch with him.

She glanced at the digital clock on her wall. "Do you mind waiting a few minutes while I wrap up here?"

"Not at all."

Oscar made his way to the sofa and sat down. He picked up a copy of *Atlanta* magazine, which featured one of her designs on the cover, crossed his legs, and started flipping through the pages.

He hadn't said a word about her hair, but she tried not to think about the omission too much. She continued working, every now and again glancing up to examine his profile. He appeared engrossed in the article.

It was strange to have him sitting in her office, the two of them calm and friendly instead of getting ready to rip each other's throats out. A peculiar sensation settled in her stomach. Almost as if…

She shook her head.

No.

Not going there. Not going to envision a life and events that could never be. Plenty of acrimony existed between her and Oscar, and truthfully, she didn't know if she could trust him. Toe-curling sex and a temporary truce meant nothing.

She hazarded another quick glance at his strong profile before returning her attention to the document before her.

What if it was all an act to get back into her good graces? To fool her into a sense of security, to only yank it all away again?

Stop.

Sighing, Sylvie set aside the document. She could hardly

concentrate, and it was lunchtime. She might as well go to lunch with Oscar.

She rose from the chair, and he tossed the magazine to the coffee table and stood. "You ready?" he asked.

"Yes. Where are you taking me?"

"It's a surprise."

A little smile flitted across his lips and then manifested in his eyes. That smile was going to be the death of her for sure. Already her heart was racing.

"What are you up to, Oscar Brooks?" Sylvie tucked her purse under an arm and walked over to him.

"Wait and see."

He still hadn't commented on her hairstyle. Had he not noticed? She brushed hair off her shoulder and made sure to run her fingers through the thick tresses. Still nothing.

She clenched her teeth in irritation. Granted, she hadn't known he'd show up today, but he could at least *comment* on her hairdo.

"Are you ready?" she asked, in a snippy tone.

Oscar slipped an arm around her waist and leaned in to whisper, "Glad you wore your hair down today. You look very sexy, my love."

Sylvie swallowed back the surge of elation that filled her chest. She lifted one shoulder in a casual shrug. "I'm trying something new," she said.

Oscar brushed aside her hair with his nose and kissed her cheek and neck. Pinpricks of desire attacked her skin in the same spots where his moist mouth landed. Two nights with the man and she was nothing but raw nerves.

"Oscar, my goodness." She playfully slapped his chest. "We are not young twenty-somethings anymore."

"Why should they have all the fun?" he asked with a frown.

Sylvie laughed. "What am I going to do with you?" She practically floated on air. Too much time had passed since she'd experienced such lightness of being.

"I could think of a few things," he said, eyes filled with mischief.

Oscar tucked her arm around his, and they walked out of the office together.

CHAPTER 8

*O*scar took her to a restaurant in a northwest suburb, but not just any restaurant. She recognized the exterior the minute they pulled up. This part of the metro Atlanta area contained a high concentration of Brazilians, flourishing with restaurants and bakeries that offered authentic cuisine. Oscar's mother had been friends with the owners of this particular establishment.

As the hostess escorted them to a quiet corner, Sylvie murmured, "It's been a long time, but I remember this place." The restaurant served a mixture of Italian, Portuguese, and Spanish dishes, the ambiance providing a nice dining experience without being pretentious.

The small dining room was filled to capacity during the lunchtime rush, but because Oscar knew the owner-chef, they received a well-appointed table in a corner.

"You remembered," he said.

"Of course." Sylvie spread a cloth napkin on her lap. "You brought me here on our second date."

"To impress you." He sat beside her instead of across the table, a fondness in his eyes that made her choke up, and she looked away before she fooled herself into thinking she saw more than fondness.

"You didn't have to impress me," she said, smoothing the napkin across her thighs.

"You came from a wealthy family. I had to pull all the strings I could to prove to you that you weren't making a mistake."

And yet she still did, didn't she? Although she wasn't so sure anymore. The old feelings he evoked were not strange—they were achingly familiar.

Oscar ordered a diverse menu of items, everything served family style with a robust Madeira wine.

As dishes continued to arrive, Sylvie exclaimed, "This is too much!"

"It's never too much," Oscar told her.

"*Coma! Coma!*" The female server said.

"You heard the woman. Eat." Oscar winked and dug in.

They started with *caldo verde,* a kale and potato soup, and moved on to other dishes—shrimp in a white wine sauce, chicken piccata, all served with a warm basket of Brazilian cheese bread, *pao de queijo.*

Sylvie ate as much of the tasty food as she could. At one point, the owner came out, a tall man with a bulbous nose set in an angular face. He'd inherited the restaurant from his father. He and Oscar hugged like long lost brothers, and after he said a few words to Sylvie, disappeared into the kitchen again.

By the time the meal was over, Sylvie surveyed the mostly empty plates and grimaced. "How do you expect me to go back to work after this?" she asked.

Oscar chuckled. "Don't go back to work. Spend the rest of the afternoon with me."

"You know I can't do that." She shook her head. She wanted to. The temptation was strong. "I have responsibilities."

"I'm going up to Lake Lanier. Join me."

"You completed the boat sale?"

"All done. An afternoon on the lake is my reward."

"I can't just leave my work. I run three businesses."

"You're the boss, aren't you?"

"Yes, but…"

He angled his body closer. "But what? So what if you miss one day? It's not even an entire day, only half a day. It's Friday afternoon, and the weekend is around the corner. I'm sure your employees would be happy for a break from the boss, don't you think? And besides, are you telling me that as the owner of three companies, you can't take off the afternoon and enjoy yourself? Everything will fall apart?"

"No…" she said slowly.

"I didn't think so. You're a brilliant woman, and I'm sure you've trained your staff well."

"Now you're purposely flattering me to get your way." She set the napkin on the table. "What are we going to do there? If you could just be more specific…"

"If you could just let me handle the details." His voice became firmer. "You run your businesses however you want. I respect your abilities. You're capable in that respect. But for the rest of the afternoon, for only a few hours, let me take control. Let me steer. You sit back and enjoy the ride. Can you do that?"

Warmth blanketed her hand, and she looked down to see his hand covering hers. The differences between them were stark. His fingers were blunt and thick, his skin a light color of coffee mixed with copious amounts of cream. Her much darker fingers were slender, the nails painted an almost translucent pearl color.

She slid her hand from beneath his. She couldn't think clearly when Oscar touched her. She brushed a crumb from atop the tablecloth, giving herself time to make a decision. He was essentially asking her to give up control to him, but he had no idea how difficult that would be. It wasn't only about letting him steer. She felt as if she would lose a little bit of her heart. A little bit of her sanity.

"I rented a luxury pontoon boat. We could cruise out on the lake and enjoy the afternoon and watch the sun set. What do you think?"

"So you had this planned from the beginning?"

"Something like that."

Sylvie swallowed. "What's going on, Oscar?" she asked quietly. "How long will we continue to do this?"

The smile died on his face. "Until we get tired."

Or until *he* got tired, and then she'd be left alone with nothing but memories. Again. "I don't know…" Sylvie shook her head, feeling weepy and glancing away.

She was slipping, falling, tumbling back under his control and going back to a place she knew all too well.

A place where she was dependent, not independent. Weak, not strong. Afraid instead of fearless. Vulnerable instead of invincible. That was how loving this man made her feel.

He set an arm cross the back of her chair. "Why can't we simply enjoy ourselves?" he asked.

"We can."

"Then come with me. It's just for the afternoon."

Despite her reservations, she wanted to spend more time with him. Take the risk. Ignore the danger. She was, after all, a risk taker in every other avenue of life.

Sylvie lifted her gaze. "All right," she said softly. "Just for the afternoon."

* * *

THEY SPENT the entire weekend together. Late Sunday morning they went to brunch and then an art auction, where Sylvie bought several paintings, one for herself and two others as gifts.

Now Oscar lay in Sylvie's huge bed in his boxers, two

pillows between his back and the tufted headboard, and Sylvie wrapped in the sheet on her back, using his stomach as a pillow. The sex drunk expression in her honey-colored eyes made her look drowsy, and was a powerful ego stroke.

"I cannot believe I had sex with my ex-husband again."

"No one is more surprised than your ex-husband," Oscar said, his voice filled with amusement.

Sylvie didn't respond right away, running the back of her fingers through the hairs on his chest. A few grays were sprinkled among them. "Look at this gray hair. You're getting old," she said.

"The only reason you don't have any gray is because you color yours." Oscar combed his fingers through the soft ebony hair spilling across his stomach and the sheets.

"Because I refuse to get old. Ever."

He chuckled softly. "You're never going to change, are you? Your vanity is astounding," he teased.

"It's not vanity. It's good planning. I moisturize with a four-hundred-dollar-per-ounce night cream every night. It has excellent anti-aging properties."

He laughed. "So I'm going to be the creepy old guy with the sexy young wife?"

She smiled, and he knew he'd pleased her by describing her as young and sexy.

"We're no longer married," she reminded him.

"Oh, right. Girlfriend, then."

"Yes, I'm afraid so. You will be the creepy old man." She turned so her cheek rested on his belly while she looked up at him. "When do you go back to Miami?" she asked.

"Don't know. There's nothing in Miami for me and no reason for me to go back. Maybe ever."

"Your life is there."

"Maybe not. Maybe my life is here." He brought her hand to his lips and kissed the finger where she used to wear his rings.

She outlined his lips with a finger. "You always say the right things, Oscar." He saw the doubt in her eyes and realized she wasn't completely convinced. He still had work to do.

"I mean it, Sylvie."

She sat up abruptly. "I'm starving, since we skipped dinner. Let's see what Trevor prepared for us."

Sylvie donned a nightie and negligee set in palest yellow and slid on a pair of fluffy sandal slippers. She watched Oscar pull up his trousers and then she led the way through the condo to the kitchen. Standing in the midst of the glistening appliances, she didn't know where to begin. Searching for spoons, she opened one drawer, but found it filled with all sorts of kitchen gadgets. After opening and closing another drawer, that one filled with knives, she said, "We should probably call Trevor, because—"

"We're not calling Trevor or anyone else. Sit," Oscar said.

"I'm sure that I can get—"

"Sit, Sylvie, before you hurt yourself or mess up Trevor's system. The man has everything in a certain order, and you know he doesn't like you messing around his kitchen."

Sylvie set her hands on her hips. "You and Trevor seem to forget that I am the one in charge in this house."

Oscar placed both hands on her shoulders. "Yes, my love, you are the one in charge, but if anything happened to Trevor or any one of your household staff, you would be completely help-less, so let's not play that game." He kissed her nose and then set about opening drawers and getting utensils together.

"You make it sound so awful."

"That's because it is. You're used to being taken care of." He shot a look over his shoulder. "Sit."

Sylvie flounced over to a stool at the island and watched him remove the food from the warm oven. He heaped beef short ribs in a red wine sauce onto each plate. A potato galette and sautéed spinach accompanied the fragrant dish.

"One thing I do know is where the wine is kept. I can get that, at least."

She retrieved a bottle of red wine from the temperature-controlled wine room beside the kitchen. When she returned, Oscar had already placed the decanter and two glasses on the island. She poured them each a glass and munched on grapes while he finished preparing their plates.

Finally, he placed the meals on the island and joined her.

"I can't believe I'm eating this late," she murmured, although the food smelled delicious. The scent of thyme and rosemary, used to season the meat, filled the kitchen. "You're the one who always eats at god-awful hours of the night." Sylvie cut into a short rib. The meat melted on her tongue in a burst of flavor.

"Me?" Seated beside her but catty-corner, Oscar frowned.

"Yes, you. You always get hungry after sex."

Oscar laughed heartily. "That's ridiculous. What are you talking about?"

"It's true. I noticed it years ago, right after we were married. Why do you think there were always platters of your favorite snacks in the refrigerator? Those platters didn't magically make themselves." Sylvie placed a piece of the galette in her mouth. "Mmm. These potatoes are divine."

Oscar stared at her. "You prepared those snacks for me?"

"Well, I didn't, but I always made sure the housekeepers fixed something for you. Don't you remember, our old housekeeper, Jackie, always made those sausage and cheese balls you liked, or the beef samosas? Things like that?" Sylvie continued eating her meal.

"I do remember," Oscar said slowly.

Sylvie noticed he hadn't touched his plate. "The food is quite delicious, darling. Are you not hungry?"

"I'm hungry, I..." His brow furrowed. "I didn't know you did that, Sylvie."

"Well, of course I did. Half the time the children raided the refrigerator for leftovers. Good heavens, there were times I worried they had tapeworms. Especially Stephan and Reese—you know how those two can eat. I couldn't have you getting up in the middle of the night with nothing to eat."

"I could have eaten potato chips or nuts or..." His voice trailed off when she glowered at him.

"Absolutely not."

"So the sandwiches—"

Sylvie waved her fork. "The sandwiches, the samosas, the sausage and cheese balls you love so much. All of it."

Oscar's eyes softened and he leaned over, kissing her hard on the mouth. While she sat there stunned, he cut into the galette on his plate. "You're not half bad."

She beamed at him. "Is that supposed to be some type of compliment?"

He grinned and continued eating.

They both laughed.

Their conversation, eating together, and laughing like a normal couple made Sylvie's chest warm at the perfection of the moment. But every time she looked at Oscar for too long, with his curly hair, the thin crinkles at the corners of his eyes, and the tempting curvature of his mouth, her heart hurt.

Then words emerged at the tip of her tongue—words she wanted to say but pride wouldn't allow. They simply tortured her by going around and around in her head in a slow loop.

Don't leave me again.

But she didn't say the words. She just kept smiling and laughing.

And being strong.

CHAPTER 9

*O*scar extended his stay in Atlanta and, except for a day when he flew back to Miami, spent every evening with Sylvie. It was almost like old times. They talked late into the night until they fell asleep, her head resting on his shoulder, her body pressed against his and covered in a white nightie not nearly as soft as her smooth skin. Each time he woke up in the middle of the night and listened to her even breathing, he wondered if their time together was all a dream. Was he really holding Sylvie in his arms? Then he'd squeeze her closer, to make sure, before drifting off to sleep again.

So far they'd kept their burgeoning relationship low-key, but last night he'd taken her to an upscale eatery that served an eclectic menu of Asian and Latin-inspired dishes, followed by an excellent opera performance at the performing arts center in Cobb County where they'd run into an acquaintance. Tonight they'd truly gone "public" by attending an event together. Surprised but familiar faces greeted them and offered congratulations on their reconciliation.

Standing against the wall, with an arm resting on a bistro table, Oscar could see the gala was a success, and as usual, Sylvie wowed the guests with her style and grace. At ease in her element, she held court in the center of the room. Instead of having to work the room, person after person approached, seeking her attention.

Her brilliant smile shone like the diamonds in her ears and around her neck, the elegant black evening gown—one of her own designs—was stunning in its simplicity. At the moment, the mayor had her ear, but Sylvie's eyes roamed the room until they settled on Oscar. He lifted his glass of whiskey in a silent salute. She smiled and continued her conversation.

His sons Reese and Stephan approached, both wearing white tuxedoes.

"Hello, Dad," Reese said.

Oscar clapped him on the arm. "Finally back from New York, I see."

"Finally," Reese said, with a grin.

"So…you and Mother, huh?" Stephan's light brown eyes, which matched his mother's, landed with curiosity on Oscar's face.

Oscar grinned. "Yes, it appears so." His gaze found Sylvie, who'd transitioned into an earnest conversation with an actor.

"When did that happen?"

Oscar drained the glass and set it on the table. "Not too long ago. We've been taking things slowly, getting to know each other again."

"Huh."

Oscar frowned. That was hardly the response he'd expected from Stephan, and Reese appeared to be equally as somber.

"So how long is this going to last?" Reese asked.

"Excuse me?" Oscar looked from one to the other.

"You're only here for a short time, right? Then you'll return to Miami, and then what? You and Mother going to work on your relationship long distance, or will your departure mean the end?"

"Your mother and I are adults and can handle our own affairs. We'll figure out the details."

A look passed between the brothers, reinforcing the sense that Oscar and Sylvie's reconciliation displeased them.

Reese spoke next. "The last thing we want is for Mother to get hurt."

"We haven't seen her like this in a very long time. She's glowing," Stephan said.

"You say that as if it's a bad thing," Oscar said with a laugh. "Maybe she's enjoying herself, enjoying my company."

"That's just it. We're certain she's enjoying herself," Stephan said.

"So then what's the problem?" Oscar demanded. He hadn't seen his sons in weeks, but the direction of the conversation irritated him.

"You know how Mother is. She's fragile."

"Your mother is the strongest person I know."

Stephan shook his head vehemently. "Then you don't know her. She's fragile, and we don't want to see her hurt. Not again. Not by you, or anyone else."

What the hell?

"Are you threatening me?" Oscar laughed a little bit, but neither Reese nor Stephan joined in the laughter.

"Yes," they said in unison.

"Don't play games with her heart. Don't hurt her again," Reese said.

Mouth agape, Oscar watched his sons stalk across the room. They went directly to Sylvie, and her eyes lit up when she saw them. Although he couldn't hear the sound of her voice, he imagined her murmured excitement at their arrival. They each took turns giving her a hug and kiss, and when she pointed in his direction, they nodded—indicating they'd already seen and spoken to Oscar.

Oscar flagged down a server for another drink and then

smiled at a friend who approached—one he hadn't seen in a while. The local socialite was someone he and Sylvie used to spend time with, back when they were married.

"You and Sylvie?" she said. "You old dog, you. Congratulations!" She gave him a brief hug.

Oscar grinned and entered into an animated conversation with his friend. As they talked, uneasiness stirred in the bottom of his stomach. All along he'd blamed Sylvie for the end of their marriage, but had he also played some part in its demise?

During those few minutes with his sons, he'd learned two valuable pieces of information. First, Stephan and Reese's loyalty to their mother was absolute. Second, they thought he had hurt her and were still angry at him about it.

* * *

OSCAR STOOD in the doorway of Sylvie's dressing room. The mostly white space popped with color from an extensive wardrobe of clothes, shoes, and accessories. Her high heels had been removed and sat in front of the storage island, while she took out the left earring in front of the vanity mirror.

"Aren't you going to get undressed?" she asked, slanting a glance at him.

"No, I just want to watch you."

He enjoyed watching her, and from the little smile that remained on her lips, she enjoyed being watched.

"Would you like to go to brunch tomorrow? Kayak Restaurant has an extensive selection, and it would be the perfect excuse to get out of the house and sit on their patio and enjoy a nice meal." She lifted an eyebrow.

"Sounds like a good idea."

"Perfect. Oh by the way, I spoke to Simone about Cameron and told her I won't meddle in her relationship."

Oscar crossed his arms over his chest. "That's a good start, but you should meet with him again, in a different setting this time. Give him a chance. Get to know him."

"Perhaps I will, and when I do I'll also make sure he understands that if he hurts Simone, I will destroy him and his little nightclub." She reached for the other earring.

Oscar pressed a hand to his head and sighed. "No, Sylvie. You won't do that. That's not how this works."

"Why can't I destroy him if he hurts my daughter?"

"Because Simone is an adult, and if they break up, they go their separate ways. Period. She only needs you to comfort her afterward. No one needs to be destroyed."

She sniffed. "No one hurts my babies."

"*Sylvie.*"

"I heard you." She set the earring on the vanity beside its twin but didn't look at him.

"You don't always have to retaliate. The kids are grown."

"I will take your opinion under advisement." She reached for the latch on her bracelet next. "I don't want her to get hurt, that's all. You know how Simone is. She's so sensitive. Her heart is too big."

She could almost be talking about herself. Sylvie donated millions every year to her family's foundation and other charitable organizations, supporting worthy causes around the country and the world. In addition, she funded documentaries that addressed a variety of social issues. She exemplified a living, breathing example of the mantra her family had lived by for years—that they were in a unique position to leave the world in a better state than they found it, and it was their moral duty to do so.

"I didn't leave because I stopped loving you," Oscar blurted. The words came out of him in an unexpected rush.

Sylvie paused, an expression of uncertainty crossing her face. "Okay," she said, setting the bracelet on the table.

She reached back for the latch on her necklace, but Oscar

moved quickly and replaced her fingers with his. Watching her reflection, he said, "I left because we were hurting each other. Too much."

Her hands remained at her sides, eyes connecting with his in the mirror. Oscar placed the necklace on top of the vanity and rubbed his hands up and down Sylvie's bare arms.

"You hated me," she said.

"Hated what we'd become," he said quietly. "I never hated you."

"I couldn't tell."

"I never stopped loving you, Sylvie." His voice had turned into a hoarse whisper.

The dewy sheen in her eyes twisted his heart.

"You don't mean that," she said huskily.

He gently squeezed her soft skin. "I do. At first I couldn't admit my feelings, but I can't tell you how many times I questioned the children for news of you. I wondered what you were doing. What great business feat you had accomplished. The more intimate questions, the ones I didn't dare ask, were who were you dating and why hadn't you remarried?"

A watery smile crossed her lips. "I questioned the children for news of you, too, hoping I wasn't being too obvious," Sylvie said in a soft voice.

"What are you saying?"

"I suppose—" She broke off, inhaled, swallowed.

Oscar waited, his own breath arrested in his lungs, pervasive tension in his chest.

Sylvie turned to face him but focused at a point on his upper torso. "I've been so angry. So hurt. For so long." She fingered a button on his shirt and looked up at him. "I never stopped loving you, either."

Oscar's arms swept around her waist on a sigh of relief as he drew her closer. "We can do this, can't we?"

She nodded. "I think so."

"We'll get it right this time."

She nodded again, and he kissed her mouth. Sylvie's arms closed around his neck as she lifted on the toes of her bare feet, pressing her soft body against his. No other woman felt as perfect in his arms. No one else made the blood surge in his veins the way she did. Thirty years from now, this was the woman he wanted by his side.

Oscar rubbed his hands up and down the curve of her spine, then lower to her soft bottom. He drizzled soft kisses to the corner of her mouth and sucked on her lower lip. Her moans made his body hard, and his lips became eager to taste every inch of her skin. He backed her into the bedroom, their mouths clinging together, arms locked around each other.

When they stood in front of the bed, Oscar lifted his head and let the back of his hand brush against her temple. He still couldn't believe he was here with her again. His heart became full and near to exploding in his chest.

"Oh, Oscar," she whispered, her gaze running over his face. Her fingers followed suit, touching the corners of his eyes and brushing his hair. The love was there for him to see, unveiled, shining in her eyes. "How I've missed you." Her upper lip trembled and her voice shook.

His heart flew high in his chest, as buoyant as his spirits in that moment. Oscar lowered the zipper of the dress and eased it down her shoulders, eager to show how much he loved her, and for much too long, how much he'd missed her, too.

CHAPTER 10

"*Is* there anything else?" Sylvie looked around the small boardroom at the team of seven, anxious to get out of there. The impromptu meeting at the end of the day with the fashion team had taken longer than expected, but now everyone had their assignments and she was confident they were well on their way to being ready for the upcoming breast cancer awareness fundraiser and fashion show.

Everyone at the table shook their head.

"Since there are no further questions, I'll excuse myself from this project moving forward. Roselle is the new point person. Questions, comments, and suggestions should be funneled through her. I don't want to hear about it unless the sky is falling, is that understood?"

Nods all around.

"Wonderful. Have a good weekend, everyone."

The group stood, gathering up notepads and electronic tablets, and filed out of the room. Roselle remained behind.

In the past few weeks, she'd gone through quite a transformation. Her hair, cut in a layered bob, glistened and moved when she did. The gray pallor in her cinnamon-brown skin had been replaced with red undertones, giving her complexion a refreshed, natural appearance. Her sticklike frame had filled out some, so that the wine-colored slacks and cream blouse hung on her body in a flattering way.

She picked up a green smoothie from the table. "Jacques called. He has a new face he wants to send for next week's go-see. He thinks you'll love her."

"Jacques always thinks I'll love his models." Sylvie pursed her lips and stood. "But a fresh face might be perfect for the new print campaign." She walked out of the room and Roselle followed. "Have her come in. You'll be here, of course?"

"Of course," Roselle confirmed.

"Perfect. I'll let you and Nick handle the go-see and choose the models you think best fit with our brand. The three of us can meet afterward and discuss your impressions. You and Nick can handle that, can't you?"

The additional responsibility made Roselle's eyes glow. "Yes, Miss Johnson. Thank you." No gushing. Just a simple thanks and a faint smile of appreciation.

"Wonderful. Have a good weekend."

Roselle smiled and then walked away, her steps more confident, her strides sure. They still had work to do, but she'd come a long way in a short time.

Sylvie approached Inez. "Any messages?"

"Business-wise, nothing that can't wait until Monday, but you did receive a message from Mr. Brooks that he would be running an hour late for dinner this evening."

The delay was actually perfect. The extra hour gave Sylvie time to wrap up a few more items on her to-do list and make a stop on the way home.

She left the office thirty minutes later. Her driver took her to a specialty store where she picked up a gift she'd ordered for Oscar—nine stainless steel whiskey stones set in a pine box, which she'd had engraved with his name on top of it. An inexpensive gift, but one she thought he'd appreciate and could make good use of when he enjoyed the occasional nightcap.

"You can take the night off," Sylvie said to the driver, as she exited the limo onto the sidewalk. "I'm in for the rest of the evening."

"Thank you, Miss Johnson."

Sylvie walked toward the building. From the corner of her eye, she caught a young woman charging toward her. Doing a quick assessment, she noted anger in the woman's expression. The doorman noticed the woman at the same time and launched himself between them.

"Can I help you?" he asked, voice heavy with authority. He stood a full foot above them, with a body as wide as a wall.

Sylvie peered around him at the young woman, and recognized her as the one who'd attended the function in Miami with Oscar. The one he'd booked a separate hotel room for and sent back to Atlanta the next day.

"I need to speak to her." Her ponytail rocked when she jabbed a finger in Sylvie's direction.

"I'm afraid—"

Sylvie placed a hand on the doorman's back. "It's all right," she said, curious about why this person would be waiting outside her residence.

"If you're sure..." The doorman sent an uneasy glance in her direction.

"I am. I'm sure that...Caitlin, isn't it?—means me no harm."

He frowned, appearing unsatisfied with that response, but lumbered over to the door and crossed his arms in front of his pelvis while he kept an eye on them.

"How may I help you?" Sylvie asked.

"You stole him from me," Caitlin said.

"I beg your pardon?"

She came closer, but Sylvie stood her ground, gripping the

blue and silver gift-wrapped box in her hand, prepared to use it if need be.

"You're Oscar's ex-wife. You stole him from me."

"*Stole* him?"

"Yes." Caitlin angled her head higher. "He told me all about you. How heartless you are and how you only care about money."

Sylvie flicked her gaze over Caitlin, from her slicked-back hair to the cheap-looking pumps on her feet. "My dear, if you know who I am, then it's not very wise of you to approach me in such a manner, is it? I'm not one of your little friends. Let me make it clear who exactly I am. I am Sylvie Johnson. I have holdings in the billions. I could sell the likes of you a million times over and still have millions left. As a schoolgirl, I had more style, class, and grace than you will have in your entire lifetime. I know that must hurt quite a bit, my dear, but I'm simply telling you the truth. So please, when you approach me, have a little respect."

The young woman's lower lip trembled and her eyes flashed with a mixture of rage and pain. "You may have won the battle, but not the war. He'll be back. As a matter of fact, I bet you don't know I saw him recently. Did he mention that? He gave me this." She extended her wrist to show off a diamond bracelet. "The only reason he's with you now is because of your money. Up until we saw you in Miami, I made him happy."

"Well, you must not have made him very happy if just the sight of me caused him to be done with you." Sylvie leaned in closer and whispered, "If I were you, I wouldn't tell anyone that."

Caitlin let out a low growl. "It's true what he said about you. You're a heartless, raging bitch!"

Sylvie gave the young woman a slow, frosty smile. She'd been called much worse in her lifetime. "Let me explain to you about being a raging bitch. A raging bitch can crush you

66

beneath her three-thousand-dollar stilettos and press"—she demonstrated with her left foot—"until there is nothing left but your empty, flattened carcass. You, my dear, are as insignificant as a worker bee. I, on the other hand, am a queen bee. Do you know what the queen does?"

Sylvie didn't wait for an answer.

"The queen controls. Everyone follows the queen. Even the man who calls her a heartless, raging bitch. Because they can't stay away. The pheromones make me irresistible—spelled with a P-H instead of an F, in case you need to look it up when we get through here. Run along." She made a shooing motion with her hand. "Go back to whatever hole you slithered out of. Because you obviously have me confused with someone who gives a damn. And I don't."

She stalked toward the building with her head held high. The doorman swung the door wide and she glided through.

CHAPTER 11

The minute Oscar stepped off the elevator into Sylvie's penthouse, he knew something was wrong. Unnerving quiet and stillness in the air warned him about trouble to come before he saw her face.

She sat on the loveseat in the sitting room, legs crossed, with a gift-wrapped package beside her. When he entered, a steely expression filled her honey-colored eyes.

"Are you all right?" he asked.

"You won't believe what happened when I arrived at home this evening." Her voice sounded oddly upbeat. Cartoonish in its cadence.

"What happened?" Oscar asked slowly, cautiously. He came farther into the room.

"I ran into your girlfriend, Caitlin. Right outside the building."

Oh no. His shoulders dropped in dismay.

Although he initially thought Caitlin had accepted his dismissal after their dinner, she'd started calling him again last week. Finally, a couple of days ago he'd told her to stop calling once and for all. He didn't think she even cared about him. She was more interested in the extravagant lifestyle he'd temporarily exposed her to.

"Nothing to say?" Sylvie said.

"Are you going to listen to my explanation?" Oscar asked.

She shot to her feet. "Have you been seeing her while you've been seeing me? Did you buy her a diamond bracelet?"

He lifted a hand to calm her down. "Sylvie, let me explain."

"The answer is yes or no. It's very simple."

"The answer is not simple at all. The answer is complicated. Yes, I saw her—"

"*You saw her?*" Her eyes widened. "While you've been seeing me?"

"The first week or so after I arrived in Atlanta, I met with her. Briefly."

"Was that before or after you kissed me?"

Dammit. Any answer he gave made him sound guilty, and he was sorely tempted to lie. "After."

"Well…" She swallowed and fisted a hand on her hip. "You've become a bit of a playboy in your old age. You have an older, wealthy lover and a young, nubile whore. How wonderful for you."

"She's not a whore." Oscar immediately regretted the response when her eyes widened accusatorially. "What I mean—"

"What you mean is I should not say anything about your girlfriend."

"You're blowing this whole thing out of proportion."

"Am I blowing the diamond bracelet out of proportion, too?"

"The jewelry was a parting gift, given to her weeks ago. Something to say goodbye, that's all."

"I thought you said goodbye to her in Miami."

"I did, but she called, and I thought it was rude to ignore her."

"You're such a kindhearted man. If only all sugar daddies were as generous as you, the world would be a better place."

"Stop it."

"Stop it? What else are you hiding from me?"

"I wasn't hiding anything. She and I are done."

"Then what was she doing here? How many others are there?"

"There are no others," Oscar insisted.

"You will not make a fool of me, Oscar Brooks! How dare you! How dare you come here and speak to me about your feelings and love. Love? You know nothing about love. You're nothing but a con artist! I'm not even sure we're back together at this point."

"What?" Self-control slipped between Oscar's fingers. "Why do you think I've been here all this time? I don't have any business in Atlanta. I'm here for you—because of you." He let out a disgusted breath. "You're not going to let me explain, are you?" he said through gritted teeth. "This isn't about Caitlin. You were waiting for me to screw up. Because when I screw up, it proves you were right all along."

"What does that mean? Are you leaving?"

"I should. I should walk out of here and leave your difficult ass all alone."

"Do it! I don't care!" she screamed.

"You don't care?" Bitterness curled Oscar's hands into fists, and he laughed hollowly. "Good to know. Because I'm done. I'm not putting up with this shit." Oscar swung around toward the door.

"Go! J-just leave me."

Oscar paused in the doorway, shoulders taut. Beneath the angry words, he'd heard strain in her voice.

"Go, Oscar. Since I'm such a horrible person, no one can stand to be around me."

Oscar closed his eyes and quickly counted backward to calm

his fury. He must be insane. He needed his head examined, but walking out the door was the last thing he wanted to do. Giving up was the last thing he wanted to do. He'd done it before and been miserable for years, the only true joy in his life the time he spent with his children and grandchildren, who always reminded him of the woman he'd been in love with for more than thirty years.

No matter how much he'd tried to fight it, the truth had been there all along. Sylvie Johnson was the beginning and the end for him. No one else sent him through the same gamut of emotions. Yes, he was insane. Because for him, a life without Sylvie was a helluva lot worse than a life with her. Life without her was no life at all.

Oscar turned slowly back around and took a good look at his ex-wife.

She clutched her hands to her chest, her body deathly still, as if she held her breath. The same way he did.

"Loving you is no walk in the park. You are dramatic and moody and difficult as hell." Sylvie winced, and he took a few steps into the room. "You have a big heart, but that doesn't mean you're not spoiled by the excess you were born into. And for some reason, I love you, with all of that drama and moodiness and excess. It's like a damn curse. Maybe I'm crazy, but God help me, I love you the way you are. I wouldn't change a thing."

Tears filled her eyes.

"I'm only going to say this once. Caitlin means nothing to me. We had a brief relationship—we never even slept together—that ended when I saw you in Miami. She knows that. She's jealous of you and came here to cause trouble. The bracelet was a gift, because I felt guilty about dumping her so suddenly." He took another two steps forward. "If we're going to do this—and by the way, we are—you have got to stop fighting me. I can deal with your moodiness. I can handle you being difficult. But what I will not tolerate is you fighting me over nonsense. Stop testing me. You taught the same thing to our daughters, and it's a recipe for disaster. When love is strong, you don't have to arbitrarily test it. You need to trust that it's sound. Trust, Sylvie. Otherwise, why are we even doing this?"

She licked her lips. "So you're not leaving?"

"I'm not leaving, but you have to meet me halfway. Starting now."

She took two tentative steps, but Oscar couldn't bear the slow movements, and he rushed forward in impatience, pulling her into his arms.

She clung to him and pressed her face into his neck, taking a deep breath.

"Why can't you be nice, hmm?" he asked, kissing her temple.

"You're the only one who can make me be nice."

Oscar cradled her in his arms, rubbing her back, and she purred her contentment. After a short while, he cupped her face in his hands. "I need to say something. Listen carefully, and don't say a word."

"Okay," she whispered.

"See, I said not a word, and you still have to talk."

She pulled in her lips and he smiled.

"Are you listening?"

She nodded.

He spoke slowly and quietly, looking deeply into her eyes. "I love you. I am not going anywhere. Stop pushing me away. Okay?"

She nodded, and the way she looked at him, he knew this time she believed him.

"I'm sure you were able to handle Caitlin," he said, raising an inquiring brow. Knowing Sylvie, she'd probably eviscerated the young woman. "You may speak now."

She sniffed. "I have no idea what you saw in her in the first place, but I made sure she knew not to come around here ever again. It was actually quite fun," she said with a smug smile.

"You're a mess, you know that?"

"I know, but I'm trying to be better."

"Well, try harder."

She smiled. "Okay. For you."

"What am I going to do with you?"

Her face lit up into a broader smile, and she rested her head against his chest. His arms closed tight around her, and she let out a relieved breath. "Keep me."

"Why would I do that?" He caressed her back, squeezing her tight. Holding her in his arms felt good. Right. Perfect.

"I'm the best thing that ever happened to you."

"Says who?" he asked against her ear. He kissed her temple.

She tipped back her head to look up at him. Her eyes smiled into his. "You did. Don't you remember? You used to tell me so all the time."

CHAPTER 12

Sylvie and Oscar headed toward the bedroom. Oscar carried a glass of whiskey with a couple of whiskey stones in it, and Sylvie leaned on his arm, giggling at a joke he'd repeated from the movie they'd watched in the entertainment room.

The elevator opening and closing in the vestibule sounded down the hall.

"Mother?" High heels thumped on the wood floor.

Sylvie and Oscar went around the corner to find Simone standing in the middle of the corridor. Their daughter's eyes widened and her mouth fell open. "Stephan and Reese said the two of you had reconciled, but I said no way. They would have told us. Is—is it true?"

Her eyes flicked over Oscar's silk pajama bottoms. Sylvie pulled the silk robe tighter around her body.

"Is anybody going to explain this to me? You two hate each other," Simone continued.

"We've decided to give marriage another shot," Oscar said, gazing lovingly down at Sylvie.

"Why? You said she's cold and callous," Simone said.

The smile died on his face. "I guess I'm attracted to cold and callous."

"You said she doesn't have a soul."

"Okay, Simone, that's enough! Don't talk about your mother in that way."

"I didn't make those comments, you did!" Simone reminded him.

"Nonetheless, it's not necessary."

"So, when are you getting remarried?"

They smiled at each other.

"When we're ready," Sylvie said. They'd discussed a possible fall wedding, but for now, were not in any rush. They needed time to plan the right event, and she wanted to design the perfect gown for the ceremony.

Simone pressed a hand to her forehead. "I feel like I'm in the Twilight Zone."

"Is it really so hard to believe your father and I are reconciled?" Sylvie asked. "We've worked out our differences."

"Isn't this what you wanted?" Oscar said.

"Yes, but I'm worried you're going to kill each other."

Oscar looped an arm around Sylvie's neck, and she pressed back against him. "We've learned our lesson. Older and wiser. I love this woman. I'm not letting her go again." He kissed the side of her neck.

"Oscar, behave."

"Mother, you're blushing. You never blush."

Sylvie laughed self-consciously. "Well, it's your father's fault."

Simone stared at them in disbelief.

"Sylvie has something she wants to tell you," Oscar said, dropping the binding hand.

"Oh, yes." Sylvie cleared her throat. "I think it would be a good idea for you and me and Cameron to have lunch."

"Umm..." Simone tucked hair behind her ear and glanced at Oscar.

"Oh, for heaven's sake, don't look at your father. I'm not going to say anything inappropriate to your boyfriend. I simply want to meet with him again and get to know him, that's all."

Simone raised a brow. "That's all, Mother?"

"Yes. I'm giving him a chance to let me know what his intentions are toward you."

"And you want the chance to make a better impression?" Simone asked.

"Why would I—" Oscar poked Sylvie in the back. "Ow." She glared at him, and he raised an eyebrow at her. "I mean, um... yes. I would like the opportunity to make a better impression. I don't want Cameron to feel unwelcome, so I thought sitting down and talking would be a good idea. That's not so bad, is it?"

"I guess not."

"Do you think he would be willing to meet for lunch?"

"I'm sure he'll meet with you. Cameron's a great guy, and you'll love him."

Sylvie took a deep breath. "I'm sure I will, as long as he's good to you."

"He is. You know he is. I've told you so." Simone came forward and hugged Sylvie. "Thank you, Mother," she whispered, before withdrawing.

Sylvie clasped Simone's face between her hands and tenderly smoothed back her daughter's hair from her face. "I only want the best for you. You know that."

"I know."

Sylvie gave her a hug.

When they separated, Oscar took Sylvie's hand. "All right, Simone. We're going to bed. See yourself out." He pulled Sylvie along behind him toward the bedroom.

Sylvie glanced over her shoulder. Her daughter stood there with her mouth slightly open. Sylvie grinned through the biting of her lip and scampered along behind Oscar.

* * *

Sylvie knew the moment Oscar's warm body left hers. She moaned and shifted in the dark.

"Sorry, my love," he murmured. "I'm going to get something to eat." He left the bed and she rolled onto her back, watching him pull on the pajama pants he'd discarded when they made love earlier. "Do you want anything?" he asked, pausing with his hand on the doorknob.

A streak of light landed on Oscar, perfectly highlighting his features. The dusting of hair that covered his firm chest. The swath of gray through the rumpled dark curls on his head. His handsome face, struggling under the vestiges of sleep.

"No, I'm fine, darling," Sylvie replied.

Now that the man she loved had returned, she didn't want—or need—anything else.

ALSO BY DELANEY DIAMOND

Check out the other books in the Brooks Family series and get to know the other family members!

Simone Brooks meets and falls in love with nightclub owner Cameron Bennett, but will her wealth and status drive a wedge between them? Find out in A Passionate Love.

Can a sudden, single kiss get Oscar Brooks and Sylvie Johnson back together after fifteen years apart? Read about their reconciliation in Passion Rekindled.

After a scary break-in at her apartment, will Ella Brooks find love in an unexpected place, the second time around with Detective Tyrone Evers? Follow their romantic journey in Do Over.

Malik Brooks is celibate. Can he resist the fireworks between him and relationship expert Lindsay Winthrop when they enter into a fake relationship? Read their funny, sexy path to love in Wild Thoughts.

Bad boy Stephan Brooks is willing to risk it all for fashion director Roselle Parker. Find out why in Two Nights in Paris.

The biggest mistake Reese Brooks ever made was hurting the woman he loved. Will he ever be able to win Nina Winthrop's love again? Or is it too little too late? Read their story in Deeper Than Love.

* * *

Audiobook samples and free short stories available at www.delaneydiamond.com.

ABOUT THE AUTHOR

Delaney Diamond is the USA Today Bestselling Author of sensual, passionate romance novels. Originally from the U.S. Virgin Islands, she now lives in Atlanta, Georgia. She reads romance novels, mysteries, thrillers, and a fair amount of nonfiction. When she's not busy reading or writing, she's in the kitchen trying out new recipes, dining at one of her favorite restaurants, or traveling to an interesting locale.

Enjoy free reads on her website. Join her mailing list to get sneak peeks, notices of sale prices, and find out about new releases.

Join her mailing list
www.delaneydiamond.com

facebook.com/DelaneyDiamond
twitter.com/DelaneyDiamond
bookbub.com/authors/delaney-diamond
pinterest.com/delaneydiamond